D1543740

www.FlowerpotPress.com
DJS-0810-0198
ISBN: 978-1-4867-2104-7
Made in China/Fabriqué en Chine

The
Book
of
Hugs

Written by Tim Harris
Illustrated by Charlie Astrella

Hi, I'm Teddy Bear Tim
and I LOVE hugs!

I love monkeys, too. I think that is because monkeys love two things—hugs and bananas—and I love hugs and bananas, too. This book is not about bananas; it is about hugs. I asked my monkey friends to help me with this hug book. Maybe when we're done we'll go get a banana.

We're here to teach you all about hugs.
There are a lot of different kinds of hugs.
There are happy hugs, sad hugs, fast
hugs, slow hugs, monkey hugs, and even
bear hugs. The one thing that makes all
hugs the same is that they are all about
sharing love.

If you want to give someone a hug there are three simple steps.

Step 1: You should ask first. You only give someone a hug if they want a hug.

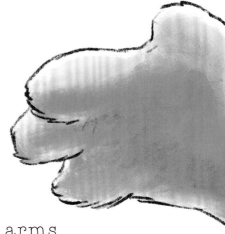

Step 2: You should open your arms really wide, but not too wide, so you can still wrap them up in your hug.

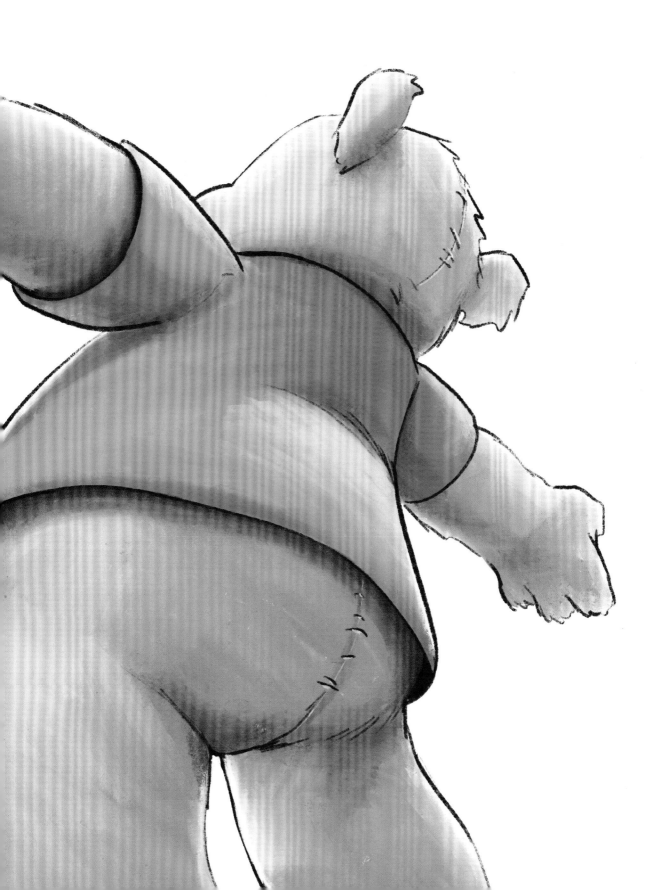

Step 3: Once you wrap someone up in a hug, you should hold them nice and tight, but not too tight. A hug should feel cozy and comfortable.

That is all there is to it! Now you can go give some hugs.

If you see someone who is happy and you know they want a hug, you can run into each other's open arms for a great big hug. This is one of my favorites.

If you see someone who is sad, you can ask if they want a hug and then give them a soft hug full of love. That might help them feel better.

Sometimes if you are in a hurry, you can give a quick hug for about five seconds.

Sometimes if you have time,
you can give a slow hug for
about ten seconds.

If you are friends with a monkey or just know a monkey hugger, then you can get a hug that feels like you are all wrapped up in their monkey arms.

And if you know a bear, or even a teddy
bear, then you can get a big squeeze of a hug.
Just hope they don't squeeze too tight.

Whatever you do and whenever you hug, just make sure you put a whole lot of LOVE in your hug. The LOVE is the most important part.

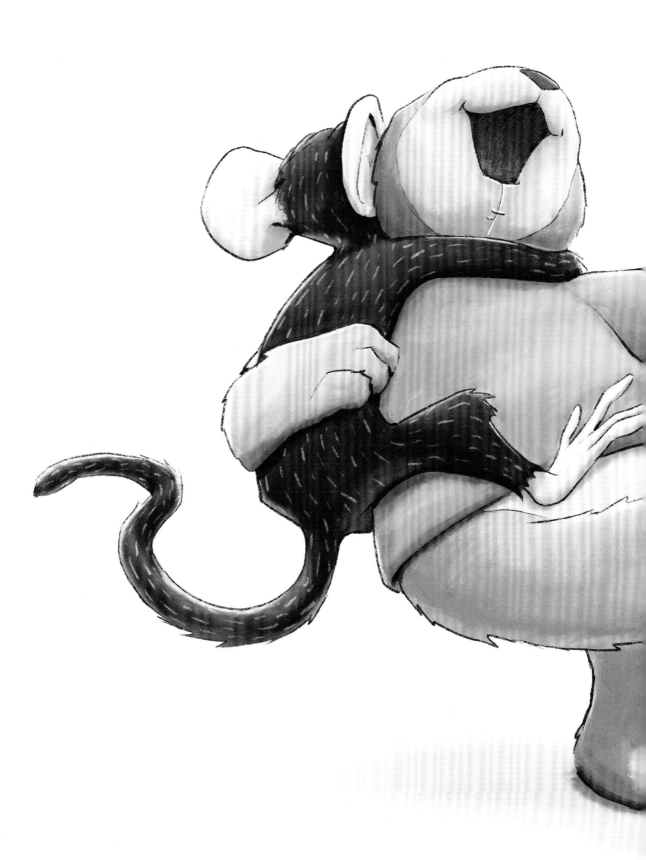

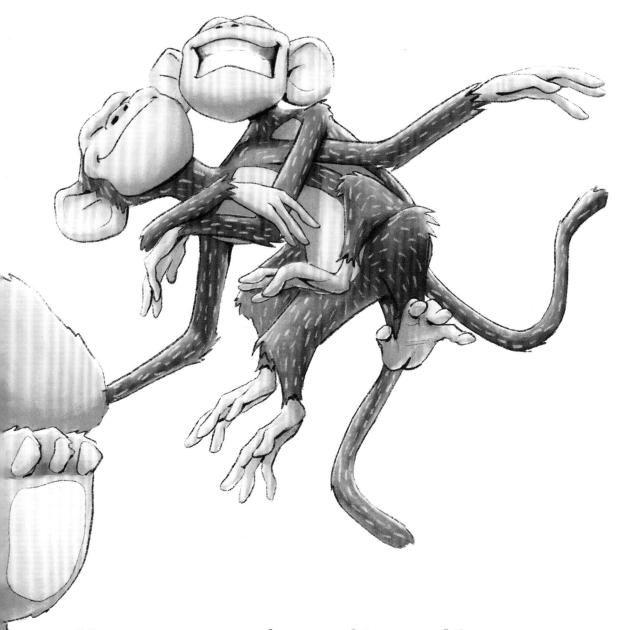

Now you are a professional hugger like my monkey friends and me. I hope you start to love hugging as much as we do. Maybe you can start practicing with whoever read this book with you! (Don't forget to ask first!)

So long! I am off to hug the world!

And maybe get a banana...

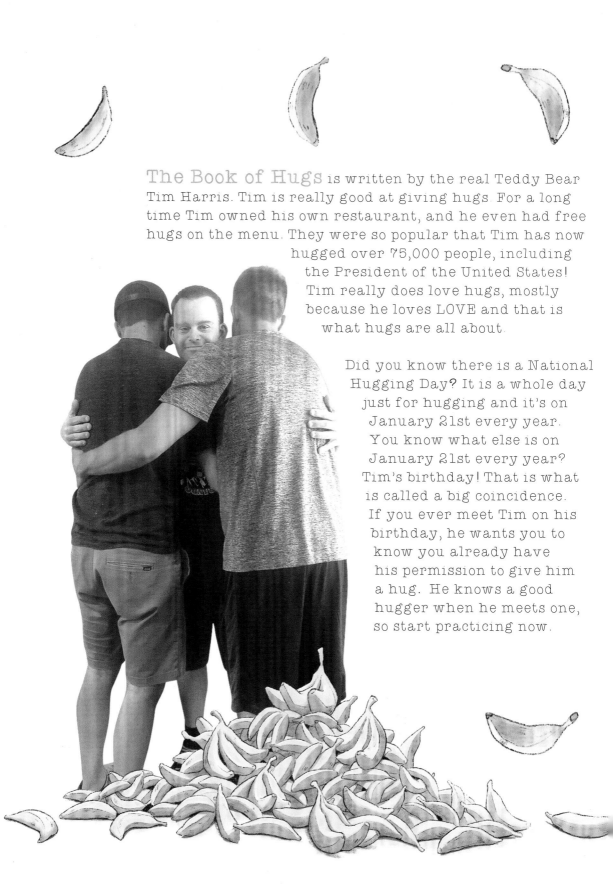

The Book of Hugs is written by the real Teddy Bear Tim Harris. Tim is really good at giving hugs. For a long time Tim owned his own restaurant, and he even had free hugs on the menu. They were so popular that Tim has now hugged over 75,000 people, including the President of the United States! Tim really does love hugs, mostly because he loves LOVE and that is what hugs are all about.

Did you know there is a National Hugging Day? It is a whole day just for hugging and it's on January 21st every year. You know what else is on January 21st every year? Tim's birthday! That is what is called a big coincidence. If you ever meet Tim on his birthday, he wants you to know you already have his permission to give him a hug. He knows a good hugger when he meets one, so start practicing now.